Balboa Press books may be ordered through booksellers or by contacting:

Balboa Press
A Division of Hay House
1663 Liberty Drive
Bloomington, IN 47403
www.balboapress.com
1 (877) 407-4847

Because of the dynamic nature of the Internet, any web addresses or links contained in this book may have changed since publication and may no longer be valid. The views expressed in this work are solely those of the author and do not necessarily reflect the views of the publisher, and the publisher hereby disclaims any responsibility for them.

Any people depicted in stock imagery provided by Getty Images are models, and such images are being used for illustrative purposes only. Certain stock imagery © Getty Images.

ISBN: 978-1-9822-4374-6 (sc)
ISBN: 978-1-9822-4375-3 (e)

Library of Congress Control Number: 2020903676

Print information available on the last page.

Balboa Press rev. date: 02/28/2020

BALBOA.PRESS
A DIVISION OF HAY HOUSE

# DEDICATION

I WISH TO DEDICATE THIS BOOK TO MY AMAZING WIFE, KARINA, AND OUR THREE BEAUTIFUL DAUGHTERS: CASSIE, DESTINY, AND VICTORIA.

YOU ARE ALL A DREAM COME TRUE WITH A LOVE THAT NEVER FAILS.

# TOTI & TITO'S MAGICAL ADVENTURES

## BY DEAN HAYEK

SOME TIME AGO, THERE WAS A
MAGICAL LITTLE MOUSE.

**HIS NAME WAS TITO!**

IT WAS A VERY COLD AND WINDY NIGHT. TITO HAD NO PLACE TO STAY.

INSIDE THE HOUSE WAS A LITTLE
GIRL. HER NAME WAS TOTI.

TITO KNOCKED ON
THE DOOR, "KNOCK,
KNOCK, KNOCK"!

TOTI HEARD THE
KNOCKS AND
SAW TITO BY
THE DOOR.

TOTI QUICKLY
BROUGHT TITO INSIDE AND KEPT
HIM WARM BY THE FIREPLACE.

THEN TITO TOOK OUT HIS MAGICAL BLANKET THAT HE KEPT INSIDE HIS SUITCASE.

HE WAS VERY HAPPY
NOW THAT HE WAS WARM.

HIS SMILE MADE THE
MAGICAL BLANKET GLOW.
TOTI LOOKED VERY
SURPRISED AND THEN SHE SAID, "WOAH!"

TITO LIFTED HIS MAGICAL BLANKET AND INSIDE WAS A SMALL SHINING LIGHT!

TOTI WENT UNDER
THE MAGICAL BLANKET AND NOW
EVERYTHING BECAME BRIGHT!

ALL OF A SUDDEN,
THEY WERE AT A
BEAUTIFUL PARK.
THEY PLAYED FOR A
VERY LONG TIME.

AFTER A WHILE TOTI
AND TITO WENT UNDER THE
MAGICAL BLANKET AND THEY
WERE NOW BACK AT HOME.

IT WAS LATE AT NIGHT AND
IT WAS TIME TO SLEEP.

FROM THEN ON,
TOTI AND TITO BECAME THE
BEST OF FRIENDS.

Printed in the United States
By Bookmasters